FANGBONE!

THIRD-GRADE BARBARIAN

THE EGG OF MISERY

MICHAEL REX

G. P. PUTNAM'S SONS AN IMPRINT OF PENGUIN GROUP (USA) INC.

G. P. PUTNAM'S SONS

A DIVISION OF PENGUIN YOUNG READERS GROUP.

PUBLISHED BY THE PENGUIN GROUP.

PENGUIN GROUP (USA) INC., 375 HUDSON STREET, NEW YORK, NY 10014, U.S.A.

PENGUIN GROUP (CANADA), 90 EGLINTON AVENUE EAST, SUITE 700,

TORONTO, ONTARIO M4P 2Y3, CANADA (A DIVISION OF PEARSON PENGUIN CANADA INC.).

PENGUIN BOOKS LTD, 80 STRAND, LONDON WC2R ORL, ENGLAND.

PENGUIN IRELAND, 25 ST. STEPHEN'S GREEN, DUBLIN 2, IRELAND (A DIVISION OF PENGUIN BOOKS LTD).

PENGUIN GROUP (AUSTRALIA), 250 CAMBERWELL ROAD, CAMBERWELL, VICTORIA 3124, AUSTRALIA

(A DIVISION OF PEARSON AUSTRALIA GROUP PTY LTD).

PENGUIN BOOKS INDIA PVT LTD, 11 COMMUNITY CENTRE, PANCHSHEEL PARK, NEW DELHI - 110 017, INDIA.

PENGUIN GROUP (NZ), 67 APOLLO DRIVE, ROSEDALE, AUCKLAND 0632, NEW ZEALAND

(A DIVISION OF PEARSON NEW ZEALAND LTD).

PENGUIN BOOKS (SOUTH AFRICA) (PTY) LTD, 24 STURDEE AVENUE, ROSEBANK,

JOHANNESBURG 2196, SOUTH AFRICA.

PENGUIN BOOKS LTD, REGISTERED OFFICES: 80 STRAND, LONDON WC2R ORL, ENGLAND.

4/12

PUBLISHED SIMULTANEOUSLY IN CANADA. PRINTED IN THE UNITED STATES OF AMERICA.

DESIGN BY RYAN THOMANN. TEXT SET IN CC WILD WORDS.

THE ART WAS CREATED IN INK AND COLORED DIGITALLY.

T.41.5
Rex

LIBRARY OF CONGRESS CATALOGING-IN-PUBLICATION DATA IS AVAILABLE UPON REQUEST.

ISBN 978-0-399-25522-9

1 3 5 7 9 10 8 6 4 2

SGL 55672

$16.00

TO MARK,
WHO HAD LONG BLACK HAIR AND
CAME FROM A DIFFERENT LAND . . .

4

OUT GOES THE FOOD!

IN GOES THE EGG!

DO NOT FORGET THE SCROLL!

HA! HUMAN SCUM! YOU WILL NOW FEEL THE WRATH OF DROOL!

OOH! STEWED MAGGOTS!

WE MUST GO!

UK—

7

IN OUR WORLD . . .

FANGBONE! IT'S TIME FOR SCHOOL.

FANGBONE!

FANGBONE?

10

WHAT KIND OF BEAST?

A WHITE TITAN RAZOR DRAGON!

A... *DRAGON?*

THE MOST POWERFUL DRAGON OF ALL.

A REAL DRAGON? LIKE WITH WINGS AND CLAWS?

AND BREATHING FIRE AND STUFF?

YES. IT IS MINE TO HATCH AND RAISE. BUT A DRAGON SPITS FIRE, IT DOES NOT BREATHE IT.

WHOA! WE GOTTA GO OR WE'LL BE LATE FOR SCHOOL!

I AM NOT GOING.

I MUST STAY HERE WITH THE EGG. GO WITHOUT ME, BILL THE BEAST.

BRING THE EGG TO SCHOOL. YOU CAN SIT ON IT THERE.

I'LL SIT ON IT TOO.

HMMMM . . .

YOU STILL HAVE TO PROTECT THE BIG TOE, REMEMBER? YOU NEED HELP!

YOUR PLAN MAKES SENSE, BILL. THERE IS SAFETY IN NUMBERS.

At School...

GOOD MORNING, BOYS.

HI.

GREETINGS, MISS GILLIAN.

FANGBONE, WHY ARE YOU SITTING ON A BACKPACK?

WHAT THE HECK IS AN EXTINCTION PAGEANT?

EACH CLASS WILL BE ASSIGNED AN EXTINCT ANIMAL TO LEARN ABOUT. WE ARE GOING TO BUILD A MODEL AND PUT ON A SKIT THAT EXPLAINS HOW THE ANIMAL LIVED AND WHY IT BECAME EXTINCT.

ARE YOU GOING TO WRITE THE SKIT?

NO. THE CLASS WILL WRITE IT TOGETHER.

ARE YOU GOING TO BUILD THE MODEL?

NO. YOU WILL DO ALL OF THE WORK BY YOURSELVES!

WE CAN'T DO THAT STUFF!

YEAH! IT WILL BE TERRIBLE IF WE DO IT. WE'RE GOING TO LOSE.

17

THE . . . DODO BIRD!

BEEP! BEEP! DOES NOT COMPUTE!

DODOS ARE STUPID!

THAT'S NOT A REAL BIRD!

YES IT IS! THEY WERE SUPER FAT AND COULDN'T FLY AND IT WAS REALLY EASY FOR HUNTERS TO CATCH THEM.

THAT'S ABSOLUTELY RIGHT, BILL. HOW DID YOU KNOW THAT?

I DON'T KNOW. I LIKE NATURE SHOWS.

WELL, BILL, SINCE YOU KNOW SO MUCH ABOUT DODOS, YOU SHOULD BE TEAM LEADER FOR THIS PROJECT!

UH . . . OK.

HELLO, EGGY. HOW WAS YOUR DAY?

WHY ARE YOU TALKING TO THE EGG?

I WANT THE DRAGON TO KNOW MY VOICE.

WHY?

SO IT WILL KNOW WHO ITS MOMMY IS WHEN IT HATCHES.

GREETINGS, EGG!

SHHHHHH... IT'S A BABY.

GREETINGS, EGG.

AT BILL'S HOUSE...

GET BACK, BEAST!

19

AWAY FROM THE EGG!

OR I WILL STRIKE!

HEY! YOU FOUND OUR CAT. SHE'S USUALLY SLEEPING IN A CLOSET.

IT LIVES IN YOUR HOME?

YEAH. SHE'S OUR PET.

CAN IT DEFEND YOU? CAN YOU MAKE BOOTS FROM ITS FUR? WHAT PURPOSE DOES IT SERVE?

HER PURPOSE IS TO BE CUTE.

ISN'T THE DRAGON GOING TO BE YOUR PET?

PET? NO! THE DRAGON WILL BE A WARRIOR!

HELLO, MISS JELLYBEAN. HOW'S MY WIDDLE WELLYBEAN?

21

22

23

WHERE . . . WHERE DOES ALL OF THIS FOOD COME FROM?

TRUCKS BRING IT FROM FARMS AND FACTORIES.

IT'S LIKE A DREAM . . . I HEAR SPIRITS SINGING!

THAT'S JUST THE RADIO.

WHILE SEARCHING FOR HIS BRIDE-TO-BE, STONEBACK MET THE QUEEN OF SNAKES. SHE TOLD STONEBACK THAT ZIZELLA WAS BEING HELD IN THE DUNGEON OF CASTLE SCALPHEAD.

STONEBACK STORMED THE
CASTLE AND SMASHED THE
DOORS DOWN!

ZIZELLA WAS NOT THERE!
INSTEAD, IT WAS THE KING OF
SNAKES AND HIS ARMY!

ZIZELLA HAD PAID THE SNAKE
LORDS TO KILL STONEBACK.

SHE HAD NEVER WANTED TO
MARRY HIM AND HAD BEEN
RUNNING FROM HIM FOR AGES.

STONEBACK FOUGHT LIKE A DEMON!

HE BEGAN TO JUMP UP AND DOWN, SMASHING
THE SNAKES AND CRACKING THE GROUND!

THE QUEEN OF SNAKES WAS SO
SAD TO SEE HER ARMY CRUSHED,
SHE BEGAN TO CRY . . .

AND SHE NEVER STOPPED!

HER TEARS FILLED THE CRACKS, AND THE RIVERS BEGAN TO FLOW.

WOW . . . DID THE QUEEN HAVE A CROWN?

YES.

WAS THERE GLITTER ON THE CROWN?

NO, BUT THERE WERE JEWELS AND DIAMONDS AND GOLD AND SILVER!

NO GLITTER? LAME.

OK, EVERYBODY, WE STILL HAVE A LOT OF WORK TO DO FOR THE PAGEANT—

BILL, WHY ARE YOU SITTING ON THE BACKPACK NOW? IS YOUR BUTT WOUNDED TOO?

HE IS HEALTHY. HE IS HELPING ME.

HELPING YOU WITH YOUR *BUTT*? IS YOUR *BUTT* BETTER?

STOP TALKING ABOUT MY BUTT.

LISTEN CLOSELY, MY ARMY! IN THE BACKPACK IS AN EGG . . . AN EGG OF THE WHITE TITAN RAZOR DRAGON. I MUST HATCH IT. IT WILL HELP ME PROTECT THE BIG TOE OF DROOL.

A DRAGON? A *REAL* DRAGON?

YES.

DUH, DRAGONS AREN'T REAL.

THEY ARE IN SKULLBANIA.

FOR THOUSANDS OF WINTERS, THE WHITE TITAN RAZOR DRAGONS WATCHED OVER THE CLANS. WHEN DROOL'S EVIL ARMIES STARTED TO SWEEP ACROSS THE LAND, THE DRAGONS FOUGHT ALONGSIDE THE CLANS.

BUT DROOL USED HIS WICKED MAGIC TO TURN THE WHITE TITAN RAZOR DRAGONS INTO BLACK DWARF FUZZ BUNNIES! THE BUNNIES WERE TERRIFIED OF FIGHTING AND USELESS IN BATTLE.

BOING!

BOING!

THOSE POOR LITTLE BUNNIES HAD TO FIGHT?

YES.

AWWWW... POOR BUNNIES.

A LONE DRAGON HID FROM DROOL IN THE MOUNTAINS OF CRANIA AND REMAINED UNCHANGED. I HAVE THE EGG OF THE LAST WHITE TITAN RAZOR DRAGON.

AWESOME!

AWESOME!

THIS SCROLL WILL TEACH US TO TAKE CARE OF OUR DRAGON.

COOL. IT CAME WITH INSTRUCTIONS. CAN I HELP?

ME TOO!!

CAN I SIT ON IT?

YES, WE WILL ALL DO OUR PART!

AND WE ALL HAVE TO DO OUR PART FOR THE PAGEANT!

WE WILL HATCH THE DRAGON AND RAISE IT TO BE A PART OF OUR ARMY. BUT NO ONE ELSE MAY KNOW!

41

SO, WHAT ANIMAL DID 3G GET FOR THE PAGEANT?

WE'RE DOING THE DODO.

THAT MAKES SENSE! DODOS MAKING A DODO!

HA! HA! HA! HA!

MY BUTT!

IN CLASS 3G...

WHAT'S THAT?

IT'S A LIST OF NAMES FOR THE DRAGON.

BUT YOUR JOB IS MAKING THE MAP OF AFRICA.

I'LL DO THAT NEXT. WHAT DO YOU LIKE BETTER, "CUTIE-CUTE" OR "SWEETIE-SWEET"?

WHAT ABOUT "BITEY-BITE"?

WHAT ABOUT "FLAMETHROWER"?

HOW ABOUT "FLAMEY-FLAMETHROWER"?

OH... JEEZ...

BILL THE BEAST, ARE YOU ILL?

YOUR FEET... SMELL... SOOOOO BAD...

YES! THEY ARE FRAGRANT AND BOLD. THEY REEK OF A LIFE FILLED WITH TRIUMPHANT BATTLES!

THERE WAS ONCE A GREAT WARRIOR NAMED STINKPIT THE MUSTY. HE DID NOT USE A SWORD OR AX OR CLUB TO DEFEAT HIS ENEMIES. HE SIMPLY HAD TO RAISE HIS ARM, AND ENEMIES FELL.

FINALLY, STINKPIT MET AN ARMY THAT HIS PITS ALONE COULD NOT OVERCOME. FOR THE FIRST TIME IN NINETEEN WINTERS, STINKPIT REMOVED HIS BOOTS. THE SMELL WAS SO POWERFUL, IT BURNED THE ARMOR AND CLOTHES OFF THE ENTIRE ARMY . . .

. . . AND MADE THEM CRY LIKE BABIES!

THE STENCH TURNED THE FOREST INTO DESERT, AND THE ROCKS INTO LAVA!

THE ARMY, NOW CALLED THE WEEPING NAKED
OF THE BURNING ARMPIT BADLANDS, AIMLESSLY
ROAMED THE DESERT FOREVERMORE.

UH . . . I'LL BE BACK TOMORROW.
BE NICE TO EGGY . . .

WOW. EGGY'S GETTING BIGGER. ARE EGGS SUPPOSED TO GET BIGGER?

I DO NOT KNOW. THE SCROLL DOES NOT SPEAK OF IT.

THE COMPUTERS ARE BUSY. LET'S GO TO THE LIBRARY AND GET A BOOK ABOUT EGGS.

DIBBY, SIT ON THE EGG WHILE WE ARE GONE.

YES SIR! BEEP! BEEP!

NO, DIBBY. YOU HAVE TO WORK ON THE PAGEANT STUFF.

I CAN DO IT WHILE I'M EGG-SITTING.

BUT—

WE MUST TAKE CARE OF OUR DRAGON.

SIT, DIBBY.

BY YOUR COMMAND. BEEP!

IN THE HALLWAY...

HEY, DODO BOYS.

CHECK OUT OUR GIANT SLOTH.

THE HANDS ARE WRONG.

IT'S REMOTE CONTROLLED. IT'S GONNA KICK BUTT!

WHAT'S YOUR WIMPY DODO GONNA DO? MAKE A DOO-DOO?

GRRRRR!

HA! HA! HA! HA!

IN THE LIBRARY...

WHAT ABOUT THIS ONE?

THAT'S NOT REAL. IT'S FICTION. WE NEED NONFICTION.

IT IS ABOUT A DRAGON.

BUT IT'S FANTASY. WE NEED THESE, SEE? "REPTILES," "BIRDS," FARMS."

REPTILES BIRDS FARMS

ROCKED ART GOOF

DRAGONS DO NOT LIVE ON FARMS.

I KNOW, BUT . . .

DRAGON -SKY-

REPTILES

THIS IS ABOUT A DRAGON.

DO YOU SEE THE DRAGON?

YES, BUT . . .

DRAGON -SKY-

REPTILES

. . . OK.

DRAGON -SKY-

YOU HAVE MADE A WISE CHOICE, BILL.

BACK iN CLASS . . .

HEY, AREN'T YOU SUPPOSED TO BE PAINTING THE DODO?

UM . . . YEAH, BUT . . .

54

55

57

58

WHOOOOOBONK!

DOING!!

FANGBONE! THEY'RE GETTING THE TOE!

BILL! YOU TOUCHED ONE! YOU ARE DOOMED!

OH! MIGHTY GODS! HAVE WE DISAPPOINTED YOU?

HOW COULD YOU LET BILL THE BEAST, BILL THE SORCERER, BILL MY WARCHIEF, BE CURSED BY SUCH FOUL MAGIC?

I CANNOT BEAR TO WATCH HIM SUFFER AND TURN INTO A MAGGOT-COVERED WRETCH!

ALMIGHTY GODS! I WILL GIVE YOU MY LIFE, BUT PLEASE SPARE MY FRIEND!

BILL! YOU ARE NOT COVERED IN PUS-FILLED BOILS. YOUR EYES ARE NOT BLACK.

YOU HAVE NO HORNS.

YOUR TONGUE IS NOT HAIRY.

YOUR NOSE IS NOT A SNAKE.

HIS PARENTS DROPPED HIM DOWN A HOLE FILLED WITH BULL-SLUGS. BUT THE SLUGS DID NOT EAT HIM. THEY RAISED HIM AS THEIR OWN. HE BECAME PART SLUG.

HE CAN STRETCH HIS BODY OUT LONG AND THIN, AND HE LEAVES A SLIME TRAIL WHEREVER HE GOES. HE HATES HUMANS. HE WANTS TO TURN THEM ALL INTO WICKED CREATURES. THAT IS WHY HE WAGES WAR ON THE CLANS.

YOU MEAN THE WHOLE DUMB WAR WOULDN'T HAVE HAPPENED IF HIS PARENTS HAD BEEN NICER?

HMMM . . .

YOU DO NOT UNDERSTAND, BILL. HE WAS A VERY UGLY BABY!

HI.

HI! MOM, IF I WAS A REALLY UGLY BABY, WOULD YOU HAVE THROWN ME DOWN A SLUG HOLE?

NOT EVEN IF YOU HAD THREE EYES, FISH LIPS, PIMPLES AND A MOHAWK.

OF COURSE YOU WOULD NOT THROW HIM DOWN A SLUG HOLE IF HE HAD THREE EYES, FISH LIPS, PIMPLES AND A MOHAWK! YOU WOULD SELL HIM TO THE CARAVAN OF ODDNESS AND BE RICH FOR LIFE.

BUUURP!!

BILL! NO BURPING!

BURPING? WHAT IS BURPING?

THE NOISE I JUST MADE. IT'S CALLED A BURP.

AH. IN SKULLBANIA WE CALL THAT A FLUG.

BUUURP!

BILL! STOP IT! I SAID NO BURPING.

I DIDN'T. I FLUGGED.

HA! HA! HA! HA! HA! HA! HA! HA! HA!

BACKSTAGE...

THIS IS A GOOD, SAFE PLACE.

I'LL TELL MS. GILLIAN YOU'RE IN THE BATHROOM. I'LL SEND SOMEONE ELSE DOWN SOON.

YES. WE MUST KEEP THE EGG WARM. IT WILL HATCH SOON.

ARE YOU READY?

IT WILL BE A GREAT CHALLENGE.

BUT IT WILL ALSO BE A GREAT HONOR TO RAISE SUCH A CREATURE.

I WILL DO MY BEST.

75

76

IS EVERYTHING READY, BILL? YOU'RE THE TEAM LEADER.

UH, YEAH, WE'RE READY . . .

. . . MAYBE . . .

AT THE PAGEANT . . .

THE GIANT SLOTH WAS AS TALL AS AN ELEPHANT AND HAD HUGE SHARP CLAWS. THEY LIKED TO EAT LEAVES AND THEIR TEETH WERE SMALL AND BLUNT.

HERE COMES ONE NOW!

WOW.

THIS IS REALLY GOOD.

WOW.

THIS IS REALLY GOOD.

CLAP! CLAP! CL

SCIENTISTS THINK THAT EARLY MAN HUNTED THE SLOTH FOR FOOD.

AND THAT IS WHY THERE ARE NONE TODAY.

YA!

YA!

HA!

HO!

THE GIANT SLOTH BECAME EXTINCT ABOUT 10,000 YEARS AGO. THEY LIVED DURING THE PLEISTOCENE PERIOD.

THE END.

CLAP! CLAP!

CLAP! CLAP! CLAP!

THAT WAS GREAT! I CAN'T WAIT TO SEE 3G'S SKIT.

CLAP! CLAP!

CLAP! CLA

ALL RIGHT, GUYS! THIS IS IT. WE'RE NEXT. STAND THE DODO UP.

81

WELL, I'M SICK OF IT! JUST ONCE I WANT TO COME TO SCHOOL AND HAVE NO ONE LAUGH AT ME!

BILL! I UNDERSTAND THE PAGEANT IS IMPORTANT, BUT WE WILL SOON BE HATCHING THE GREATEST OF DRAGONS!

THE LAUGHTER WILL BE OVER IN MOMENTS . . . THE DRAGON WILL BE WITH US OUR WHOLE LIVES!

HEY! GUYS! SOMETHING'S HAPPENING!

RUMMMBLE!!

WHOA!!

STAND BACK! IT IS HATCHING!

CRACK!

RRRRRRRRUMBLE!

THE TOE! IT IS WIGGLING.

MAGGOT TEETH! WE HAVE BEEN TRICKED! THIS IS NOT A WHITE TITAN RAZOR DRAGON! IT IS A FEATHERED SKEEVE!

WHAT? NO DRAGON?

THIS BEAST WAS SENT BY DROOL TO STEAL THE TOE!

I CAN'T BELIEVE I SAT ON THAT EGG!

I CAN'T BELIEVE I CALLED IT "EGGY"!

GREAT! NOW OUR SKIT'S GONNA STINK, AND WE DON'T EVEN HAVE A DRAGON!

FEATHERED SKEEVES ARE STUPID!

YOU ARE AN ARMY! STOP GRUMBLING AND PREPARE FOR BATTLE!

HOW CAN DROOL CONTROL SOMETHING THAT WAS JUST BORN?

HIS MAGIC IS WICKED AND KNOWS FEW LIMITS.

90

ON THE STAGE . . .

WOW! WHAT A GREAT SHOW SO FAR. HOW ABOUT THAT GIANT SLOTH? I WOULDN'T WANT TO SIT NEXT TO HIM ON THE BUS! FOR OUR LAST SKIT, WE HAVE CLASS 3G.

THEY WILL BE TELLING US THE SAD STORY OF THE DODO BIRD. TAKE IT AWAY, GUYS!

AHEM . . . AT THE BOTTOM OF AFRICA IS AN ISLAND CALLED MAURITIUS.

IT RHYMES WITH "DELICIOUS."

HA! HA! HA!

THIS IS THE ONLY PLACE THE DODO EVER LIVED.

IT WAS A FAT BIRD THAT COULD NOT FLY.

IT HAD WINGS, BUT THEY WERE VERY LITTLE . . .

AND IT COULDN'T FLY . . .

. . . BECAUSE THE WINGS WERE LITTLE . . .

. . . AND . . . UM . . . LITTLE, TEENY, TINY WINGS . . .

AND . . . UM . . . IT COULDN'T FLY . . .

DODOS DIDN'T NEED TO FLY BECAUSE THERE WERE NO PREDATORS ON THE ISLAND. NOTHING EVER TRIED TO CHASE OR EAT THE DODO, SO IT WASN'T AFRAID OF ANYTHING. IT EVEN LAID ITS EGGS RIGHT ON THE GROUND! ONE DAY, HUNGRY SAILORS STOPPED ON MAURITIUS TO LOOK FOR FOOD. THE SAILORS BROUGHT DOGS AND RATS TO THE ISLAND. THE DOGS AND RATS ATE ALL OF THE DODO EGGS!

100

DUNCAN'S INSIDE THE SLOTH!!!

LET'S CLEAR THIS PLACE OUT—

FANGBONE! UP!

POP!

OR PEOPLE WILL GET HURT!

111

AFTER SCHOOL...

SEE YOU NEXT WEEK, LOSERS!

HEY! CALL 911! THERE'S A FIRE THAT NEEDS TO BE PUT OUT!

YOU GUYS BETTER NOT SAY ONE THING ABOUT MY UNDERWEAR!

YOU MEAN YOUR *FIRE ENGINE UNDERWEAR*?

HE'S WAITING FOR THE FIRE ENGINES TO ARRIVE! IT'S A FIVE-ALARM BLAZE! *WOOOOOOO! WOOOO!*

HA!

HA! HA!

HA! HA! HA! HA! HA! HA! HA! HA! HA!

AH, MIRTH! IT WARMS THE SOUL!

WE HAVE BEEN THROUGH MUCH. LET US GO HOME AND REST.

YOU ARE WRONG, BILL! THE TOE IS SAFE, AND MY ARMY STANDS TO FIGHT ANOTHER DAY.

AGAIN, DROOL HAS TRIED TO DEFEAT US, AND AGAIN WE HAVE STOOD AS TALL AS THE TALLEST FUNGUS BEAVER! AND WE HAVE FOUGHT AS COURAGEOUSLY AS THE DREADED HAMMER-HEADED PIGLET! WE HAVE—

BEEP! BEEP! GUYS! I MISSED MY BUS!

DO NOT WORRY. WE WILL GIVE YOU A RIDE HOME.

THE END

REAL DODO

3G'S DODO

MICHAEL REX IS THE AUTHOR AND
ILLUSTRATOR OF OVER TWENTY BOOKS FOR CHILDREN,
INCLUDING THE *NEW YORK TIMES* #1 BESTSELLER
GOODNIGHT GOON. MICHAEL HAS A MASTER'S DEGREE IN
VISUAL ARTS EDUCATION (K-12), AND WORKED AS A NEW
YORK CITY ART TEACHER FOR FOUR YEARS. HE VISITS
SCHOOLS ACROSS THE COUNTRY, AND HAS APPEARED ON
THE CELEBRITY APPRENTICE AS A GUEST ILLUSTRATOR.

MIKE LIVES IN THE BRONX WITH HIS WIFE AND THEIR
TWO BOYS.

BRACE YOURSELF FOR BOOK THREE OF
FANGBONE!
THIRD-GRADE BARBARIAN . . .

THE
BIRTHDAY PARTY
OF DREAD